NO MORE MONSTERS FOR ME!

by Peggy Parish

pictures by Marc Simont

An I CAN READ Book®

HARPER & ROW, PUBLISHERS

Weekly Reader Books offers several exciting
card and activity programs. For information,
write to WEEKLY READER BOOKS, P.O. Box 16636,
Columbus, Ohio 43216.

This book is a presentation of Weekly Reader Books.
Weekly Reader Books offers book clubs for children
from preschool through high school. For further
information write to: **Weekly Reader Books,**
4343 Equity Drive, Columbus, Ohio 43228.

Published by arrangement with Harper & Row,
Publishers, Inc.

Library of Congress Cataloging in Publication Data
Parish, Peggy.
    No more monsters for me!

    (An I can read book)
    Summary: Minneapolis Simpkin is not allowed to have
a pet, so she finds the most unusual replacement.
    [1. Monsters—Fiction. 2. Pets—Fiction]
I. Simont, Marc. II. Title. III. Series: I can read
book.
PZ7.P219No 1981   [E]   81-47111
ISBN 0-06-024657-X   AACR2
ISBN 0-06-024658-8 (lib. bdg.)

For Adele Hanna—with love.

"Not even a tadpole,

Minneapolis Simpkin,"

yelled Mom.

"And I mean it!"

"Okay, okay,"

I yelled back.

5

Mom and I always yell a lot.

But this time,

she was really mad.

And so was I.

I stamped out of the house.

I did not care

what Mom said.

I was going to have a pet.

I would take a long walk

and think about this.

So I walked

down the road.

Suddenly I heard

a funny noise.

The noise came

from the bushes.

I stopped and listened.

7

"Something is crying,

Minneapolis Simpkin,"

I said to myself.

"I will find out

what it is."

I looked in the bushes.

Was I surprised!

9

"Wow! A baby monster!"

I yelled.

I looked at the monster.

It looked at me.

Then it ran to me.

I put my arms around it.

"Don't cry," I said.

"Minneapolis Simpkin

will help you."

The monster stopped crying.

We stood there

hugging each other.

"A monster for a pet?"

I asked.

Mom never said no

to a monster.

But I never asked her that.

Will she say yes?

I needed time

to think about this.

But there was no time.

It started raining.

11

The monster did not like it.

It started bawling.

And I do mean bawling!

"Okay, okay," I said.

I grabbed the monster.

I ran home with it.

Mom was in the kitchen.

She did not see me.

But she heard me.

"Are you wet?" she asked.

"Yes," I said.

"Hurry and get dry,"

she said.

"Supper is about ready."

I ran to my room.

"So far, so good,"

I said to myself.

"But what now,

Minneapolis Simpkin?"

I shook my head.

I did not know.

"Minn," yelled Mom,

"supper is ready."

"Coming," I yelled back.

I started to go down.

The monster came, too.

"No," I said.

"You can't come."

I put the monster

in my closet.

It started bawling again.

What was I going to do?

I looked all around.

"My teddy bear!" I said.

I got the teddy bear.

"Here," I said.

The monster grabbed the bear.

It stopped crying.

17

I ran down to supper.

Mom had made a good supper.

Then I thought of something.

Monsters have to eat, too.

"Mom," I said,

"what do monsters eat?"

"Food, I guess," said Mom.

"But what kind?" I asked.

"Oh," said Mom.

"Is this a new game?"

Mom loves to play games.

So I said, "Yes."

"Let me think," said Mom.

"What *do* monsters eat?"

I was glad to let her think,

because I saw something.

I saw the monster.

"I will be right back,"

I yelled.

"I have to get something."

I had to get something, all right.

I had to get the monster hidden.

I grabbed the monster.

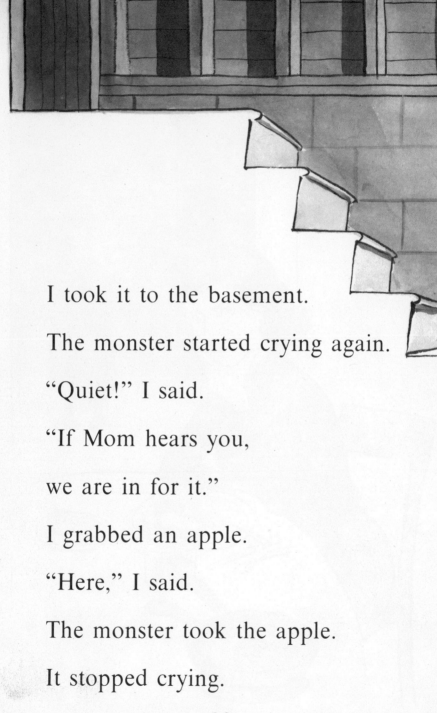

I took it to the basement.

The monster started crying again.

"Quiet!" I said.

"If Mom hears you,

we are in for it."

I grabbed an apple.

"Here," I said.

The monster took the apple.

It stopped crying.

22

I grabbed another apple.

I ran back to the table.

"Here, Mom," I said.

I gave the apple to her.

"What is this for?"

she asked.

I didn't know what to say.

But I had to say something.

"Because I love you," I said.

Mom laughed.

"Minneapolis Simpkin," she said,

"I love you, too."

Then Mom said, "Pickles!"

"Pickles?" I said.

"Of course," said Mom.

"Monsters love pickles."

"I didn't know that," I said.

25

Then I asked,

"Do you know where monsters live?"

"Yes," said Mom.

"They live in caves.

Deep dark caves."

"Gee, Mom," I said.

"You know a lot about monsters."

"I love monster stories,"

said Mom.

"I read lots of them."

Did Mom like real monsters, too?

I started to ask her.

But I didn't.

The basement door was opening.

"I will be right back, Mom,"

I yelled.

"Minneapolis Simpkin!"

yelled Mom.

"Can't you sit still?"

"Hic-cup, hic-cup!"

Oh, no!

The monster had hiccups.

"Now you have hiccups,"

yelled Mom.

"I will get some water,"

I yelled back.

"HIC-CUP! HIC-CUP!"

29

I opened the basement door.

My eyes almost popped out.

"You grew!" I yelled.

"What did you say?"

asked Mom.

"Nothing," I said.

I pushed the monster

back into the basement.

It was awful.

The monster was huge.

It was all lumpy.

"HIC-CUP! HIC-CUP!"

I got some water.

"Drink this," I said.

The monster drank the water.

The hiccups stopped.

"Minn," yelled Mom,

"please bring me

another apple."

"Okay," I yelled back.

But there were

no more apples.

Now I knew

why the monster was lumpy.

I grabbed a potato.

The monster

grabbed it from me.

I grabbed another one

and ran.

I locked the basement door.

"Here, Mom," I said.

"Minn, this is a potato,"

said Mom.

"I asked for an apple."

"Oh, sorry, Mom," I said.

"Minn," said Mom,

"why are you so jumpy?

Is something wrong?"

Something wrong?

Was it ever!

But maybe Mom could help.

So I said, "I am fine.

Tell me some more about monsters.

Where are those caves?"

"Up in the hills," said Mom.

"But don't bother

to look for one."

"Why not?" I asked.

"They are all hidden," she said.

"Only monsters can find them."

"Are you sure?" I asked.

"That is what

my mother told me,"

said Mom.

"I looked and I looked.

I never could find one."

38

I sure hoped Mom was right.

I had to get that monster home.

It was not a good pet.

Then it happened.

CRASH!

Mom jumped up.

"What was that?"

she asked.

Then she looked at me.

"Minn," she said,

"you were in the basement."

I nodded my head.

"Did you bring home

an animal?"

I nodded my head again.

"Minneapolis Simpkin!"

yelled Mom.

"I said NO PETS!"

"It is not a pet!"

I yelled back.

"Then what is it?"

yelled Mom.

I did not mean to.

I did not want to.

But I started bawling.

"It is a monster!"

I bawled.

I waited for

Mom to yell.

But she didn't.

"Oh, Minn," she said.

"You really need a pet,

don't you?"

"Yes," I bawled.

"But I want a kitten

or a puppy.

I don't want a monster."

"No," said Mom.

"A monster is not a good pet."

I stopped bawling.

"Now," said Mom

"go and close that window."

"Window! What window?"

I asked.

"The basement window,"

said Mom.

"I must have left it open."

44

I just looked at her.

I still did not understand.

"Minneapolis Simpkin!"

said Mom.

"The wind is blowing hard.

It blew something over.

That is what made the noise.

Go close the window."

I went.

There was a window open.

The potato basket

was turned over.

The potatoes were all gone.

But the monster

was still there.

It was sleeping.

I looked at it.

How would I ever

get it out of the basement?

It was getting

bigger and bigger.

48

I went back to Mom.

"I closed the window,"

I said.

"The monster is there.

But it is sleeping."

"Okay, Minn, you win,"

said Mom.

"I was wrong.

I will make a deal.

You get rid of your monster,

and you can have

a real pet.

Deal?"

"Deal!" I cried.

That monster was no pet.

But it was real.

"Good," said Mom.

"I am going to take

a long bath.

You get rid of

your monster."

"Sure, Mom," I said.

I was not sure.

But I was sure

going to try.

I woke up the monster.

"Come on," I said.

"We are going."

The monster came.

54

It had to crawl

through the doors.

And I had to push

from behind.

But we made it.

I headed for the hills.

The monster followed.

The night was very dark.

I don't like the dark.

But I had to get

that monster home.

We got to the hills.

The monster looked at them.

It made happy noises.

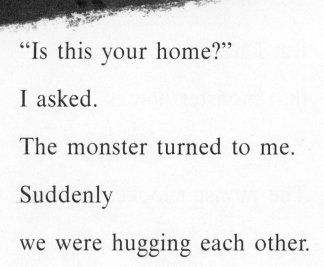

"Is this your home?"

I asked.

The monster turned to me.

Suddenly

we were hugging each other.

Then the monster

ran up the hill.

I felt good.

The monster

had found its home.

"No more monsters for me,"

I said.

I ran all the way home.

Mom was yelling for me.

I went into the house.

"Minneapolis Simpkin!"

yelled Mom.

"Where have you been?"

"Getting rid of the monster,"

I yelled back.

"That is what

you told me to do."

I started to bawl again.

Mom looked at me

in a funny way.

She hugged me.

Then I knew.

I knew Mom didn't believe

that monster was real.

But Mom kept our deal.

We went to the pet shop.

Mom really surprised me.

She bought two kittens.

"Two!" I said.

"Sure," said Mom.

"One for you,

and one for me."

"Mom," I said,

"you are okay."

"And so are you, Minn,"

said Mom.

We each took a kitten.

And we went home.